FAMOUS ANIMAL STORIES

SVEA
THE DANCING MOOSE

By LaVere Anderson

Illustrated by Richard Amundsen

GARRARD PUBLISHING COMPANY
CHAMPAIGN, ILLINOIS

Copyright © 1978 by LaVere Anderson
All rights reserved. Manufactured in the U.S.A.
International Standard Book Number: 0-8116-4862-1
Library of Congress Catalog Card Number: 77-13922

SVEA

THE DANCING MOOSE

The little moose lay under a tree in a forest in Sweden. She was alone and afraid. One of her legs hurt so much that she could not stand up.

She was hungry, and she wanted her mother. She and her mother had been running through the forest together. They were frightened because hunters were following them. Suddenly the little moose stumbled and fell. She had lain so still the hunters raced past without seeing her.

The little moose did not know how long she had been there. Why didn't her mother come back? Then the baby ears heard a rustling of dry leaves as feet moved across the forest floor. Someone was coming! She watched eagerly for her mother.

Two men came through the trees. They stopped in surprise.

"What have we here!" exclaimed one.

When she saw the men, the little moose was afraid. Her breath came fast, but she could not get up and run away. She could only lie there, trembling.

The men knelt beside her.

"Poor baby," said Torsten. "You have a broken leg." He saw how frightened she was. "We'll not hurt you," he said. His voice was kind.

"Some hunters must have killed her mother," he told his friend.

"I'll get my wagon and take her to my farm. That broken leg will mend, and she'll be safe in my barn."

He patted the small brown head. "I'll be back, little one," he said.

The baby watched the men hurry away. She felt more lonely than ever.

But soon Torsten was back. First he taught her to drink from a bottle of warm milk. The milk tasted good to the hungry little moose. Then he gently bound up her broken leg. He lifted her carefully and laid her on a bed of straw in his wagon.

"We'll soon be home," he told her.

When he put her in his barn, the little moose was no longer afraid. It was warm in the barn. She felt safe. She closed her eyes and went to sleep.

On the farm the little moose's leg soon healed. She learned to drink milk from a bucket. It was not long before she was licking grain from Torsten's hand. Then she nibbled bits of hay and grass. She grew big and strong. Torsten named her Svea.

Every day Torsten hid lumps of sugar in his pockets.

"Find the sugar, Svea," he said.

Svea nudged and nuzzled his clothes until she found the sugar.

Sometimes he held the sugar high over Svea's head.

"Now get it!" he said.

Svea danced and pranced and stretched her neck.

"You clown!" Torsten laughed. Then he gave her the sugar and petted her head. Svea nuzzled his ear and petted him right back.

Svea thought that Torsten could not do the farm work without her help. She went with him to the chicken house when he gathered eggs. She followed him to the hayfield when the hay was cut.

"Svea is my farm manager," he told his wife. "She is always at my heels."

"Not always," said his wife. "She comes to the kitchen door when I am baking bread. Today when I would not give her a slice, she danced! I could not believe my eyes! I had to feed her."

Torsten laughed aloud. "Svea doesn't think she's a moose. She thinks she's a person."

A few years passed. Svea became a full-grown cow moose. She was not pretty. No cow moose is pretty. Svea had a large hairy muzzle, short thick neck, and long knobby legs. She did not know it, but she was ugly.

One day, Svea lay near Torsten on the front porch. He read in a newspaper that the little country of Denmark had lost its only cow moose. He knew how much the Danes wanted a moose herd. Denmark lay across the sound from Sweden, and the Danish people were good neighbors.

"Now the only cow moose is dead. Unless something is done the bulls will grieve to death over her loss," Torsten read. *"Denmark must get another cow moose quickly."*

Torsten showed the newspaper to his wife.

"But how can the Danes get another cow moose?" he asked her. "Most wild animals can be captured, but moose will not be taken alive. If one is caught, it will not eat and soon starves."

Suddenly Torsten had an idea. "I know what I will do," he said.

"I'll give Svea to Denmark! She will be a gift of friendship from Sweden to the Danish people."

Torsten wrote a letter to a Danish newspaper and explained his plan. Soon everyone in Denmark knew that a cow moose was coming.

One bright morning Torsten called, "Come along, Svea. You are going to a new home."

Svea followed him to a truck. As he led her up the truck ramp, she looked at him in surprise. This was something new!

"Be a good girl in Denmark," he said. "Remember you are a gift of friendship." He fed her a last sugar lump. Then he got down from the truck, and a farm helper drove it away.

A large boat carried the truck and Svea across the sound to a little Danish town not far from Copenhagen, the nation's capital. On the boat, people crowded around the truck to look at Svea. They had never seen a moose before. Svea looked right back. She had never seen these people before, either.

Soon they reached Denmark. Thousands of Danes had come to meet Svea. Some

were from cities far away. There were newspaper reporters and photographers. There were men making movies. It was a great day for Denmark.

Stepping high on her knobby legs, Svea came down the truck ramp. Her hairy muzzle hung several inches over her flabby chin. Her brown coat was shaggy, and her tail looked like a bit of old rope. But her eyes were wide at all the attention she was getting. She loved it! Suddenly she showed her big yellow teeth in a moose grin.

She danced. She pranced. She swung her head from side to side as though she were keeping time to music. Then she turned slowly around on those long legs so that the people could admire her from all sides.

The photographers stared in amazement. "Look!" one exclaimed. "She's putting on a show!" The people laughed and clapped their hands.

Just then Svea saw a little boy eating a bun. She trotted straight to him. His mother stared in horror as Svea came toward her child. She screamed.

But Svea only nuzzled the little boy and looked hard at the bun. He broke off a piece and fed her. Then Svea nuzzled his ear.

"Why, she's kissing the boy!" someone shouted. "What a moose!"

Svea would have liked to stay right where she was, with all the laughing people. But men took her far inland to Gribskov Forest. Nobody expected to see anything more of her for a long time.

They expected her to stay deep in the forest with the bulls, lost in the rains and mist of this country by the sea.

Yes, their new moose would live happily, all the Danes said. And when the bulls found her, she would have company. Someday there would surely be baby moose.

But Svea did not live happily in Gribskov Forest. For a few days she wandered among the trees, but there was nothing for her to do. She missed the farm and the barn with her bed of sweet-smelling straw. She missed the children and the farm helpers who had played with her and fed her. Most of all she missed Torsten.

Svea was sad. Her steps slowed, and she lost her appetite.

One evening she came suddenly to the edge of the forest. Nearby stood a little house. She saw lights in the windows. Her sharp ears heard voices.

Svea's eyes grew bright as she trotted to the house. She had found people!

Behind the lighted windows Ranger Joergensen sat smoking his pipe. He was a quiet man who worked for the Royal Danish Forest Service, and he knew all about wild animals. Suddenly there was a loud noise at his front door.

The ranger's pretty daughter, Kirsten, opened the door. She looked outside, and screamed.

Ranger Joergensen grabbed his gun and ran to the door. He did not know what he'd find, but it must be dreadful to have made Kirsten scream so loudly.

What he found was Svea. There she stood, looking in the door.

"Get back, Kirsten!" he shouted. The ranger held his gun ready to shoot. He knew how dangerous a moose could be.

But this moose just stood there, looking in at the door. Then she hung her head as if to say that she was sorry for frightening Kirsten.

Ranger Joergensen lowered his gun.

"It's the new cow moose!" he growled. "But what sort of animal is she, anyway? Coming to people's doors!"

"I saw her picture and read about her in the newspaper," Kirsten said. "Her name is Svea." Suddenly she remembered that the newspaper had said Svea liked people. "Maybe she wants to be petted."

Gently Kirsten put out her hand and

patted the top of Svea's head. Just as gently, Svea nudged Kirsten's arm. Then the girl and the moose stood face-to-face, patting and nudging.

After that, Svea came to see Kirsten every morning. Because she was lonesome, she came early. Like a huge dog, she waited in the yard for Kirsten to come outside. Then she rushed to the girl, skidded to a full stop, and nuzzled Kirsten's ear. Kirsten talked to Svea, just as Torsten had done, and Svea talked back with queer rumbling noises in her throat. Sometimes she nibbled Kirsten's shoulder to show how much she loved the pretty girl.

As the days passed, Svea spent less and less time in Gribskov Forest. If the bulls had found her, she must not have liked them and so had driven them away. Nobody could say about that. Svea wandered here and there, looking for people. One day she discovered the town of Helsinge.

The town council was holding a meeting that morning. At the head of the table sat the mayor. He was a pleasant man who was a shoemaker when he was not busy being mayor.

A policeman dashed into the meeting.

"Mayor! Mayor!" he cried. "There is a moose in the street! She is threatening to hurt the children, and she has stopped all the traffic!"

The mayor frowned. "What is this, a joke?"

"No! No! It is true!" cried the policeman.

The men of the council hurried to the street.

There was a moose there, all right. All traffic had stopped because Svea stood in the middle of the road. Cars were backed up everywhere.

But Svea was not trying to hurt the children.

She was amusing them, just as she used to amuse the farm children. When the Helsinge children had first seen the great moose coming down the street, they screamed and ran away. But soon they came back to watch the antics of the funny animal. They were laughing happily as Svea danced and pranced and whirled in circles. She put on her best show. She always did her best for children.

At first the councilmen were afraid of
Svea. Moose were dangerous beasts! Yet
the men soon saw that Svea did not
mean to hurt anyone. So they tried to
chase her away.

The mayor shouted loudly and waved
his arms.

People in cars honked their horns to
scare her off.

Ranger Joergensen ran up. "I'll push
her out of the road!" he yelled. He
pushed her from one side. He pushed
from the other side. His face grew red,
and he began to pant. Svea looked over

her shoulder at him with her big brown eyes and never moved.

At last the ranger turned to a boy who was watching.

"Boy, get on your bicycle and go after Kirsten. She will know what to do. Tell her to hurry!"

When Kirsten came, she patted Svea on the head. "You must not hold up traffic like this, Svea," Kirsten said softly. "It makes trouble for people. I want you to go home now." She gave Svea's head a good-bye pat.

Svea turned and started away. As she was leaving, she sent the men a scornful look and showed them her big yellow teeth.

Svea had liked her visit to Helsinge so much that now she came to town every day. When the children saw her, they shouted, "Here's Svea!" and they ran to meet her. "Dance for us, Svea!" they cried, and Svea danced her best. She loved to hear them laugh and clap.

The mayor was angry. He said it took one policeman full time to look after the moose and straighten out the traffic jams she caused.

Newspaper reporters in Copenhagen heard about the trouble between Svea and the mayor. They came to Helsinge to watch her put on her show. Then they wrote stories for their papers.

When the Danes read the stories, they laughed in amusement.

In no time at all, Svea was the whole nation's pet.

One afternoon as Svea roamed through

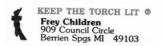

Helsinge, she saw the old people's home. It had a fine grassy yard—just right for a hungry moose to graze in. It had a nice front porch where a tired moose could lie in the sun and rest. Best of all, there were many people sitting on the porch.

So Svea stopped by to nibble a little grass. Then she went up on the porch, where she lay down for a nap. She felt right at home, for this porch was like the farm porch.

The old people were frightened. In their quiet house, they had not seen nor heard of Svea. Suddenly there was a huge dangerous beast lying by their front door. They could not even go inside. Two old ladies began to cry.

Svea sensed something was wrong. She

stood and hung her head, as if to say she was sorry she had frightened them.

So, like the children, the old people learned that Svea was a friend who had come to visit. They began to talk to her. She talked back in her rumbling voice. Some of the braver folk patted her head. Some of them moved their chairs so she would have a better place to lie in the sun.

When she left, they called after her, "Come back again."

Svea liked these new friends. She went back every afternoon for her nap in the sunniest spot on the porch.

One morning Svea reached Helsinge early. Suddenly she raised her head and sniffed the air. Yes, she remembered that smell. Somewhere there were good things to eat! Her knobby legs moved fast as she followed her nose straight to the Helsinge bakery.

Mr. Rosendahl, the baker, was busy putting fresh bread on the shelf when he heard a strange noise. He looked up toward the front of his store. Then he gasped in surprise and dropped a loaf.

There was Svea, her great ugly muzzle pressed flat against the window. Her big brown eyes looked at Mr. Rosendahl and then at his shelf of bread.

"Go away!" yelled the baker.

Svea pushed harder at the glass.

"Stop!" Mr. Rosendahl shouted. "You will break my window!"

Svea pushed again.

Mr. Rosendahl did not know what to do. He was afraid of this large fierce

creature. Still, windows cost money. Brave-
ly, he threw open the door. "Go away!"
he shouted.

Svea backed away from the window.
She hung her head.

Mr. Rosendahl began to feel foolish. "I
don't want my window broken," he said
to the moose. He went back into his
store. Svea followed him.

She sniffed at the good smell of
fresh bread. She rolled her eyes at Mr.
Rosendahl. She looked hungrily at the
loaf on the floor.

"All right," the baker grumbled. "Take
it and go away." He handed her the
bread.

Svea's strong teeth bit down on it.
She chewed with pleasure, for there was
nothing like this in Gribskov Forest.

Then she licked her hairy chops and trotted out the open door.

Next morning she was back, her nose against the window.

"No, not again!" Mr. Rosendahl said tiredly. But he knew it was no use. He went to the door and handed her a loaf of freshly baked bread.

After a week of Svea's visits, the baker had an idea. His fresh bread was too good for the moose. But he didn't want a broken window, so he would give her a loaf of yesterday's bread.

Next morning he handed Svea a stale loaf.

Chomp, chomp went her big teeth. A strange look crossed her face. She spit out the bread and stared at the baker. Quickly he handed her a fresh loaf.

"How did she know the difference?" the puzzled man asked himself.

One morning he was very busy when Svea came. Without thinking, he gave her an apple tart. Svea ate it and smacked her lips. She knew about apples! The farm children had fed them to her. After that Svea did not want bread. She wanted apple tarts.

Mr. Rosendahl could be firm when he had to be. Apple tarts were too expensive to feed to a moose. He would not do it.

Svea began to put on her morning show in front of the bakery. She danced. She pranced. She whirled round and round, tossing her ugly head proudly. The children came running to watch.

Each morning Svea looked them over,

picked a child, and gently pushed the little one inside the store. She would not let the child out unless he bought her a tart.

Sometimes a child had no money. So he turned beggar. "One tart, Mr. Rosendahl. Just one little old tart." And all

the laughing children crowded in the door shouting, "One little old tart won't hurt you, Mr. Rosendahl."

Svea always got her apple tart.

There came a day when Svea did not visit Kirsten. She did not dance for the children nor eat a tart. She lay gasping for breath in Gribskov Forest. She did not understand what was wrong, but she knew she needed help. Slowly she got to her feet. Staggering and gasping, she made her way to Kirsten's house and fell down in the yard.

Ranger Joergensen was home. One look told him that Svea was very sick. While Kirsten sat beside Svea and talked gently to her, the ranger called an animal ambulance.

Svea was taken to the big state

veterinary hospital. Three of the best animal doctors in Denmark worked to save her life. She had lung trouble, and they did not know how to cure her.

Newspapers ran stories about Svea every day. All the Danes grew worried. Many people phoned and wrote letters asking the doctors to try this medicine and that. Nothing seemed to help.

"Our moose is dying," the Danes said sadly.

Just in time, a special medicine was sent from the United States. It saved Svea. Soon she was back in Helsinge— amusing the children and annoying the mayor.

Almost every week Svea got into new trouble. And each time, someone went to the mayor's shoe shop to complain about it. Once she ate a cabbage in a man's garden. Another time she knocked down a clothesline and got mixed up in the clothes. When she chased a dog that had nipped at her heels, the frightened dog hid under a house and would not come out. His owner was afraid the dog would starve to death. And Svea was always tying up traffic.

"We must do something about that moose," the mayor told the council. "She keeps the police so busy they have time for nothing else. And I have no time to make shoes."

"What can we do?" a man asked.

"We must drive her away," said the mayor. "Who will drive her?"

The men looked at one another. Nobody said anything. It was plain that

no one wanted the job. After all, they were fond of Svea, and besides, she was a wild animal. Who knew what she would do if she were angry at being driven away?

So Svea kept on roaming through Helsinge, and almost every day she found something new to interest her. One sunny noon she stood at a bend in the road wondering what to do next. Around the bend came a car.

Wham! The driver slammed on his brakes. Just in time he saw a moose in the middle of the road!

Big Svea looked down into the small open car. Then she walked around to the driver's side and nuzzled the terrified driver's head. Her hairy muzzle was right over his face. She nosed his pocket for sugar and peered into the back seat. Then she gave the poor man a last friendly nudge and trotted off.

After that, Svea loved to stop cars, for now she knew that cars held people. She waited at the bend often and stood right in the middle of the road. She almost caused some wrecks.

Now the mayor was really angry. The council held a special meeting. There was no more talk about driving Svea away. Instead, the council wrote a sharp letter to the forestry service and said to come get Svea at once.

The service rangers came and took Svea to a game reserve in North Sealand where the bulls were. For a few days the rangers watched her. They saw she was eating natural food.

"She will soon become wild," they said.

Then suddenly Svea disappeared. The rangers hunted for several days, but they could not find her.

A week later, Mr. Rosendahl was taking some fresh bread from the oven. He heard a noise and looked up.

"Oh, no!" he said to himself. "It can't be Svea!"

It was Svea, all right, with her muzzle flat against the glass. She looked hungry, and she was pushing hard.

"Don't break my window!" yelled Mr. Rosendahl. He grabbed an apple tart and hurried to the door.

Nobody knew how Svea had found her way home, and the mayor did not care. All he cared about was getting rid of Svea once and for all.

"She cannot walk on our streets and break our laws," he said angrily. "She was sent here to start a moose herd, not to amuse children and stop cars. Since she will not stay in the forest where she belongs, she will have to go to the Copenhagen Zoo."

The council gave Svea to the zoo. The people of Copenhagen were glad. Now they could visit their moose whenever they liked. But all the children in Helsinge were sad.

At the zoo, Svea walked proudly down the truck ramp. There were many people waiting for her, so she put on a fine show. Around and around she went— dancing, prancing, tossing her head, and giving her big moose grin.

Two zoo keepers took Svea through a

high gate and across a bridge to her new home. It was a small grassy island with water around it—a wide deep moat with very steep sides.

"She'll be safe here," said one keeper.

After they left, Svea looked over her new home. There was not much to see. Svea began to feel lonesome.

She looked at the moat carefully. She looked across the water to the zoo grounds where the people were. She backed up, took a deep breath, bunched her long legs, and jumped across the nine-foot moat. Then Svea went for a walk.

She peered into parked cars. She nosed surprised people. She begged candy from a boy.

Zoo policemen ran after her, but she

paid no attention to them. She was used to policemen. She found a pond and took a bath. When she was tired, she went back to the moat. The policemen still followed her, and they were tired too.

"Thank goodness she came back here!" one of them exclaimed. "We'll have to unlock the gate and take her across the bridge. Someone must go for the key."

Just then Svea took a deep breath, bunched her legs, and jumped across the moat.

The policemen gasped. "I don't believe it!" one said. "I just don't believe it!"

After that, Svea went for a walk every day. She spent no more time on the island than she had in Gribskov Forest. She stayed where the people were, and she kept the policemen busy.

But one morning Svea did not jump the moat. Zoo keepers found her lying on the island and gasping for breath. She was sick with the old lung trouble.

This time even the best doctors and the best medicines could not help her. One sad day, Denmark's dearest animal died.

All Denmark grieved. The children in Helsinge cried. Even the mayor was a little sorry.

In Sweden, Torsten heard about it and bowed his head. "I should never have sent her away," he told his wife.

"But she had a good time in Denmark," his wife comforted him. "Remember all those stories we heard about her adventures? She had an exciting, happy life."

"Yes," Torsten nodded. He knew his wife was right. "But I'll never forget her."

And no one in Denmark has forgotten Svea either, for there was never another moose like her.